Percy B. Shelley, William M. Rossetti, Thomas J. Wise, Henry
M. Stephens, Harry B. Forman

Letters from Percy Bysshe Shelley to Thomas Jefferson Hogg

with notes by W. M. Rossetti and H. Buxton Forman

CONTENTS.

x CONTENTS.

LETTERS.

LETTERS

TO

THOMAS JEFFERSON HOGG.

———◦◦◦———

LETTER I.

FIELD PLACE,
HORSHAM, SUSSEX.
December 20th, 1810.
[*Thursday.*]

MY DEAR FRIEND,

The moment which announces your residence, I write.

There is now need of all my art; I must resort to deception.

My father called on Stockdale in

London, who has converted him to
sanctity. He mentioned my name, as
a supporter of sceptical principles. My
father wrote to me, and I am now
surrounded, environed, by dangers, to
which compared the devils who be-
sieged St. Anthony were all inefficient.
They attack me for my detestable
principles ; I am reckoned an outcast ;
yet I defy them, and laugh at their ineffectual efforts.

Stockdale will no longer do for me.
Stockdale's skull is very thick, but I
am afraid that he will not believe my
assertion ; indeed, should it gain credit
with *him*, should he accept the offer of
publication, there exist numbers who
will find out, or imagine, a real
tendency ; and booksellers possess
more power than we are aware of in
impeding the sale of any book containing
opinions displeasing to them. I am dis-
posed to offer it to Wilkie and Robinson,
Paternoster Row, and to take it there

myself; they published Godwin's works, and it is scarcely possible to suppose that any one, layman or clergyman, will assert that these support Gospel doctrines. If that will not do, I must print it myself. Oxford, of course, would be most convenient for the correction of the press.

Mr. L.'s* principles are not *very* severe ; he is more a votary to Mammon than God.

O ! I burn with impatience for the moment of the dissolution of intolerance ; it has injured me ! I swear on the altar of perjured Love to revenge myself on the hated cause of the effect which *even now* I can scarcely help deploring. Indeed, I think it is to the benefit of society to destroy the opinions which can annihilate the dearest of its ties.

Inconveniences would now result from my *owning* the novel which I have

---

* "L." is probably the initial of some Oxford printer or publisher.

in preparation for the press. I give out, therefore, that I will publish no more ; every one here, but the select few who enter into my schemes, believe my assertion. I will stab the wretch in secret. Let us hope that the wound which I inflict, though the dagger be concealed, will rankle in the heart of the adversary.

My father wished to withdraw me from college : I would not consent to it. There lowers a terrific tempest ; but I stand as it were, on a pharos, and smile exultingly at the vain beating of the billows below.

So much for egotism !

Your poetry pleases me very much ; the idea is beautiful, but I hope the contrast is not from nature. The verses on the Dying Gladiator are good, but they seem composed in a hurry. I am composing a *satirical* poem : I shall print it at Oxford, unless I find, on visiting him, that R[obinson] is ripe for printing whatever will sell. In case of that, he is my man.

It is not William Godwin who lives in Holborn : it is *John*, no relation to the other.

As to W.,* I wrote to him when in London, by way of a gentle alterative. He promised to write to me when he had time, seemed surprised at what I had said, yet directed to me as " The Reverend " : his amazement must be extreme.

I shall not read Bishop Prettyman, or any more of them, unless I have some particular reason. Bigots will not argue ; it destroys the very nature of the the thing to argue ; it is contrary to *faith*. How, therefore, could you suppose that one of these *liberal* gentlemen would listen to scepticism, on the subject even of St. Athanasius's sweeping anathema?

* "W." seems to have been some person of public note to whom Shelley had written on religious topics (especially the Athanasian creed) in a tone which, though sceptical, was also grave, and which misled "W." into supposing his correspondent to be a clergy-man.

I have something else to tell you, and
I will in another letter.

Love! dearest, sweetest power! how
much are we indebted to thee! How
much superior are even thy miseries to
the pleasures which arise from other
sources! How much superior to "fat,
contented ignorance" is even the agony
which thy votaries experience! Yes,
my friend, I am now convinced that a
monarchy is the only form of govern-
ment (in a certain degree) which a
lover ought to live under. Yet in this
alone is subordination necessary. *Man*
is equal, and I am convinced that
equality will be the attendant on a
more advanced and ameliorated state
of society. But this is assertion, not
proof,—indeed, there can be none.
Then you will say, "Excuse my believing it." Willingly.

St. Irvyne is come out; it is sent to
you at Mr. Dayrell's; you can get one
in London by mentioning my name to

Stockdale. You need not state your own; and, as names are not *now* inscribed on the front of every existing creature,* you run no risk of discovery in person, if it be a crime or a sin to procure my Novel.

How can you fancy that I shall ever think you mad? Am not *I* the wildest, the most delirious, of Enthusiasm's offspring? On one subject I am cool, toleration; yet that coolness alone possesses me that I may with more certainty guide the spear to the breast of my adversary, with more certainty ensanguine it with the heart's blood of Intolerance—hated name!

Adieu. Down with Bigotry! Down with Intolerance! In this endeavour your most sincere friend will join his every power, his every feeble resource. Adieu.

To T. J. Hogg,
    Lincoln's Inn Fields.

* An allusion probably to the brand of Cain.

D

LETTER II.

FIELD PLACE,
HORSHAM, SUSSEX.
December 23*rd*, 1810.
[*Sunday.*]

MY DEAR FRIEND,

The first desire which I felt on receiving your letters was instantly to come to London, that a friend might sympathise in those sorrows which are beyond alleviation.* That I cannot do this week; on Sunday or Monday next I will come, if you still remain in town.

Why will you add to the never-dying remorse which my egotising folly has occasioned (for which, so long as its fatal effects remain, never can I forgive myself), by accusing yourself of a feeling,

---

* The lady who was so disturbing Shelley's mind at this time was his cousin, Harriet Grove.

as intrusive, which I cannot but regard as another part of that amiability which has marked your character since first I had the happiness of your friendship? Where exists the moral wrong of seeking the society of one whom I loved? What offence to reason, to virtue, was there in desiring the communication of a lengthened correspondence, in order that both, she and myself, might see if, by coincidence of intellect, we were willing to enter into a closer, an eternal union? No, it is no offence to reason or virtue; it is obeying its most imperious dictates, —it is complying with the designs of the Author of our nature. Can this be immorality? Can it be selfishness, or interested ambition, to seek the happiness of the object of attachment? I am sure your own judgment, your own reason, must answer in the negative. Let me now ask you—what reason was there then for *despair*, even supposing my love to have been incurable?

Her disposition was, in all probability, divested of the enthusiasm by which mine is characterized : could therefore hers be prophetic ?   She might not be susceptible of that feeling, which arises from an admiration of virtue when abstracted from identity.

My sister attempted sometimes to plead my cause, but unsuccessfully. She said :—

"Even supposing I take your representation of your brother's qualities and sentiments (which, as you coincide in and admire, I may fairly imagine to be exaggerated, although *you* may not be aware of the exaggeration), what right have *I*, admitting that he is so superior, to enter into an intimacy which must end in delusive disappointment when he finds how really inferior I am to the being which his heated imagination has pictured ? "

This was unanswerable, particularly as the prejudiced description of a sister, who loves her brother as she does, might, indeed *must*, have given to her an erroneously exalted idea of the superiority of my mental attainments.

You have said that the philosophy which I pursued is not uncongenial with the strictest morality. You must see that it militates with the received opinions of the world. What, therefore, does it offend but prejudice and superstition; that superstitious bigotry, inspired by the system upon which at present the world acts, of believing all that we are told as incontrovertible facts?

I hope that what I have said will induce you to allow me still, and all the more, to remain your friend.

I hope that you will soon have an opportunity of seeing, of conversing with, Elizabeth.

How sorry I am that I cannot invite you here now! I will tell you the reason when we meet. Believe me, my dear friend, when I assert that I shall ever continue so to you. *I* have reason to lament deeply the sorrows with which fate has marked my life. I am not so deeply debased by it, however, but that the exertions for the happiness of my friend shall supersede considerations of narrower and selfish interest,— but that his woes should claim a sigh before one repining thought arose at my own lot. I know the cause of all human disappointment,—worldly prejudice ; mine is the same. I know also its origin,—bigotry.

Adieu. Write again. Believe me your most sincere friend. Adieu.*

P. B. S.

To T. J. Hogg,
   Lincoln's Inn Fields.

* Elizabeth Shelley, referred to in the foregoing letter and so often in this volume, was the poet's eldest sister, born considerably within two years of the date of his birth. At the time of this correspondence she was just over sixteen years and a half old. The next sister, Mary, was only thirteen and a half.

LETTER III.

FIELD PLACE,
HORSHAM, SUSSEX.
December 26*th*, 1810.
[*Wednesday.*]
MY DEAR FRIEND,

Why do you express yourself so flatteringly grateful to me, when I ought to experience that sensation towards *you* in the highest manner of which our nature is capable ? Why do you yet suppose that you have offended against any of those rules for our conduct which we ought to regard with veneration ?

What is delicacy ? Come, I must be severe with myself; I must irritate the wound which I wish to heal.

Supposing the object of my affections

does not regard me, how have *you* transgressed against its dictates? in what have you offended? What is delicacy? Let us define it, in the light in which you take it. I conceive it to be that inherent repugnance to injuring others, particularly as regarding the objects of their dearer preference, which beings of superior intelligence feel. In what then, let me ask again, if *I* do not think you culpable, in what then have you offended? Tell me, then, my dear friend, no more of "sorrow," no more of "remorse," at what you have said. Circumstances have operated in such a manner that the attainment of the object of my heart was impossible, whether on account of extraneous influences, or from a feeling which possessed her mind, which told her *not* to deceive another, not to give him the possibility of disappointment. I feel I touch the string which, if vibrated, excites acute pain;

but *truth*, and my real feelings which I wish to give you a clear idea of, overcome my resolve never to speak on the subject again. It is with reluctance to my own feelings that I have entered into this cold disquisition, when your heart sympathizes so deeply in my affliction. But for Heaven's sake consider, and do not criminate yourself; do not wrong the motives which actuated you upon so feeble a ground as that of *delicacy*. I do this, I say this, in justice as well as friendship; I demand that you should do *justice* to yourself,—then no more is required to give you at all events a consciousness of rectitude.

I read most of your letters to my sister; she frequently enquires after you, and we talk of you often. I do not wish to awaken her intellect too powerfully; this must be my apology for not communicating *all* my speculations to her.

F

Thanks, *truly* thanks for opening
your heart to me, for telling me your
feelings towards me. Dare I do the
same to you? I dare not to myself;
how can I to another, perfect as he may
be? I dare not even to God, whose
mercy is great. My unhappiness is ex-
cessive. But I will cease; I will no
more speak in riddles, but now quit for
ever a subject which awakens too
powerful susceptibilities for even
negative misery. But that which injured me shall perish! I even now by
anticipation hear the expiring yell of
Intolerance!

Pardon me. My sorrows are not so
undeserved as you believe; they are ob-
trusive to narrate to myself; they must
be so to you. Let me wish you an
eternity of happiness.

I wish you knew Elizabeth; she is a
great consolation to me; but, if all be
well, my wishes on that score will soon
be accomplished. On Monday night

you will see me. I cannot bear to suffer alone. Adieu. I have scarce a moment's time, only to tell you how sincerely I am your friend.*

* This letter contains an expression of great value in dealing with an important matter of textual criticism : "I feel I touch the string which, if vibrated, excites acute pain." This seems to settle the question whether Shelley was capable of using *vibrate* as a transitive verb. This he is said to have done in the *Ode to Liberty*. In the words

A glorious people vibrated again
The lightning of the nations,

the use of the word is precisely the same ; and the occurrence of the phrase in this letter leaves but little hope that he really meant the first sentence of the Ode to end at *again*.

LETTER IV.

FIELD PLACE,
HORSHAM, SUSSEX.
December, 28*th*, 1810.
[*Friday*.]

MY DEAR FRIEND,

The encomium of one incapable of flattery is indeed flattering. Your discrimination of that chapter is more just than the praises which you bestow on so unconnected a thing as the romance* taken collectively. I wish *you* very much to publish a tale ; send one to a publisher.

Oh, here we are in the midst of all the uncongenial jollities of Christmas ! When you are compelled to contribute to the merriment of others—when you

* *St. Irvyne.*

are compelled to live under the severest
of all restraints, concealment of feelings
pregnant enough in themselves—how
terrible is your lot! I am learning
abstraction, but I fear that my pro-
ficiency will be but trifling. I cannot,
dare not, speak of myself. Why do
you still continue to say, " Do not des-
pond "—that "You must not despair"?

I admit that this despair would be
unauthorized, when it was rational to
suppose that at some future time
mutual knowledge would awaken reci-
procity of feeling.

Your letter arrived at a moment
when I could least bear any additional
excitement of feelings. I have suc-
ceeded now in calming my mind, but
at first I knew not how to act. In-
decision, and a fear of injuring another
by complying with what perhaps were
the real wishes of my bosom, distracted
me. I do not tell you this by way of
confession of my own state; for I

believe that I may not be sufficiently aware of·what I feel, myself, even to own it to myself. Believe me, my dear friend, that my only ultimate wishes *now* are for your happiness and that of my sisters. At present a thousand barriers oppose any more intimate connexion, any union, with another,— which, although unnatural and fettering to a virtuous mind, are nevertheless unconquerable.

I will, if possible, come to London on Monday,* certainly some time next week. I shall come about six o'clock, and will remain with you until that time the next morning, when I will tell you my reasons for wishing to return. Adieu. Excuse the shortness of this, as the servant waits. I will write on Sunday.†

Yours most sincerely.

* *December* 31*st*, 1810.
† *December* 30*th*, 1810. No letter written by Shelley under this date is at present forthcoming.

LETTER V.

FIELD PLACE,
HORSHAM, SUSSEX.
January 2nd, 1811.
[*Wednesday.*]

MY DEAR FRIEND,

I cannot come to London before next week. I am but just returned to Field Place from an inefficient effort. Why do you, my happy friend, tell me of perfection in love ? Is she not gone ? And yet I breathe, I live ! But adieu to egotism ; I am sick to death at the name of *self.*

Oh, your theory cost me much reflection ; I have not ceased to think of it since your letter came, which was put into my hands at the moment of departure on Sunday morning.* Is it not, however, founded on that *hateful* principle? Is it *self* which you propose to raise to a state of superiority by your system of eternal perfectibility in love? No! Were this frame rendered eternal, were the particles which compose it, both as to intellect and matter, indestructible, and then to undergo torments such as now we should shudder to think of, even in a dream,—to undergo this, I say, for the extension of happiness to those for whom we feel a vivid preference,—then would I love, adore, idolize your theory—wild, unfounded as it might be. But no. I can conceive *neither* of these to be correct. Considering matters in a philosophical light, it evidently appears (if it is not treason to speak thus coolly on a subject so deliriously ecstatic) that we were not destined for misery. What, then, shall happiness arise from? Can we hesitate?

* *December 30th, 1810.*

Love, dear love! And, though every mental faculty is bewildered by the agony which is in this life its too constant attendant, still is not that very agony to be preferred to the most thrilling sensualities of epicurism?

I have wandered in the snow, for I am cold, wet, and mad. Pardon me, pardon my delirious egotism ; this really *shall* be the last.

My sister is well; I fear she is not quite happy on my account, but is much more cheerful than she was some days ago. I hope you will publish a tale ; I shall then give a copy to Elizabeth, unless *you* forbid it. I would do it not only to show her what your ideas are on the subject of works of imagination, and to interest her, but that she should see her brother's friend in a new point of view. When you examine her character, you will find humanity, not divinity, amiable as the former may sometimes be. However, I, a brother, must not write treason against my sister; so I will check my volubility. Do not direct your next letter to Field Place, only to Horsham.

To-morrow I will write more connectedly.

Yours sincerely.

LETTER VI.

FIELD PLACE,
HORSHAM, SUSSEX.
January 3rd, 1811.
[*Thursday.*]

MY DEAR FRIEND,

Before we deny or believe the existence of anything, it is necessary that
we should have a tolerably clear idea
of what it is.* The word "God," a

---

* This letter (of *January 3rd,* 1811) is of some
importance in the history of Shelley's religious opinions.
It shows that the youth who, on the 25*th* of *March,*
1811, was expelled from Oxford as author and dis-
tributor of *The Necessity of Atheism,* could, even as
late as the 3*rd* of *January* in the same year, argue
zealously in behalf :—Firstly, of the immortality of the
soul, and, Secondly, of the existence of an intelligent
"Soul of the Universe," or "First Cause," as a necessary antecedent to that immortality ; at the same time
he would eliminate the word "God" from the field of
discussion. This is sufficiently consonant with what is
propounded in the Notes to *Queen Mab,* printed (not
published) in 1813.

vague word, has been, and will continue to be, the source of numberless
errors, until it is erased from the no-
menclature of philosophy. Does it
not imply "the soul of the universe,—
the intelligent and *necessarily* benefi-
cent actuating principle? This it is impossible not to believe in. I may not
be able to adduce proofs ; but I think
that the leaf of a tree, the meanest
insect on which we trample, are in
themselves arguments, more conclusive
than any which can be advanced, that
some vast intellect animates infinity.
If we disbelieve *this*, the strongest
argument in support of the existence
of a future state instantly becomes
annihilated. I confess that I think
Pope's

" All are but parts of a stupendous whole "

something more than poetry. It has
ever been my favourite theory. For
the immortal soul " never to be able to

die, never to escape from some shrine
as chilling as the clay-formed dungeon
which it now inhabits "—is the future
punishment which I can most easily
believe in.

Love,—love infinite in extent, eternal
in duration, yet (allowing your theory
in that point) perfectible—should be
the reward. But can we suppose that
this reward will arise spontaneously, as
a necessary appendage to our nature?
or that our nature itself could be
without cause—a first cause,—a God.
When do we see effects arise without
causes? What causes are there without
correspondent effects?

Yet here I swear—and as I break
my oaths, may Infinity, Eternity, blast
me—here I swear that never will I
forgive Intolerance! It is the only
point on which I allow myself to
encourage revenge. / Every moment
shall be devoted to my object, which
I can spare; and let me hope that it

I

will not be a blow which spends itself, and leaves the wretch at rest,—but lasting, long revenge! I am convinced, too, that it is of great disservice to society,—that it encourages prejudices which strike at the root of the dearest, the tenderest, of its ties. Oh how I wish *I* were the avenger!—that it were mine to crush the demon, to hurl him to his native hell, never to rise again, and thus to establish for ever perfect and universal toleration! I expect to gratify some of this insatiable feeling in poetry.

You shall see—you shall hear—how it has injured me. She is no longer mine! she abhors me as a sceptic, as what *she* was before! O Bigotry! when I pardon this last, this severest of thy persecutions, may Heaven (if there be wrath in Heaven) blast me! Has vengeance, in its armoury of wrath, a punishment more dreadful?—Yet forgive me, I have done; and were it not for ycur great desire to know *why* I consider myself as the victim of severer anguish, that I could have entered into this brief recital.*

I am afraid there is selfishness in the passion of love, for I cannot avoid feeling every instant as if my soul was bursting. But I *will* feel no more : it is selfish. I would feel for others ; but for myself—oh how much rather would I expire in the struggle ! Yes, that were a relief ! Is suicide wrong ? I slept with a loaded pistol and some poison last night, but did not die.

I could not come on Monday, my sister would not part with me ; but I must—I will—see you soon. My sister is now comparatively happy ; she has felt deeply for me. Had it not been for her—had it not been for a sense of what I owed to her, to *you* —I should have bidden you a final farewell some time ago. But can the

* This imperfect sentence must mean " I could *not*," &c. The *that* has no business there.

dead feel ?   Dawns any day-beam on the night of dissolution ?

Pray publish your tale ; demand one hundred pounds for it from any publisher—he will give it in the event.   It is delightful, it is divine !   Not that I like your heroine : but the poor Mary is a character worthy of Heaven—I adore her ! *

Adieu, my dear friend,

Your sincere,

P. B. S[HELLEY.]

P.S.—W——† has written.   I have read his letter : it is too long to answer. I continue to dissipate Elizabeth's melancholy by keeping her, as much as possible, employed in poetry.   You shall see some to-morrow.   I cannot tell you when I can come to town.   I wish it very much.

---

* Perhaps the early verses written by Shelley, named *To Mary, who died in this opinion*, may refer to the " Mary " of Hogg's MS. novel.   There is no known person, actually connected with Shelley's biography, to whom those verses can refer.

† See *ante*, p. 7.

LETTER VII.

FIELD PLACE,
HORSHAM, SUSSEX.
January 6th, 1811.
[*Sunday.*]

MY DEAR FRIEND,

Dare I request *one* favor for *myself*
—for my own sake? Not the keenest
anguish which the most unrelenting
tyrant could invent should force me to
request from you so great a sacrifice
of friendship. It is a beloved sister's
happiness which forces me to this.
She saw me when I received your
letter of yesterday. She saw the con-
flict of my soul. At first she said
nothing: and then she exclaimed,

K

" Re-direct it,* and send it instantly
to the post ! " Believe me, I feel far
more than I will *allow* myself to express, for the cruel disappointments
which I have undergone. Write to
me whatever you wish to say. You
may say what you will on *other* subjects : but on *that* I dare not even
read what you would write. *Forget*
her ?

What would I not have given up to
have been thus happy ? † I thought I
knew the means by which it might
have been effected. Yet I consider
what a female sacrifices when she re-
turns the attachment even of one whose
faith she supposes inviolable. Hard is
the agony which is indescribable, which
is only to be felt. Will she not en-
counter the opprobrium of the world ?

---

* Shelley, it would seem, received a letter from
Hogg, and guessed that it referred to the painful
subject of Miss Grove. Elizabeth induced him to
return this letter, unread, to Hogg himself.

† "Thus happy " seems to mean *not* "so happy as
to forget her," but "so happy as to make her mine."

and, what is more severe (generally speaking), the dereliction and contempt of those who before had avowed themselves most attached to her. I did not encourage the remotest suspicion. I was convinced of her truth, as I was of my own existence. Still, was it not *natural* in her (even although she might return the most enthusiastic prepossessions arising from the consciousness of intellectual sympathy)— ignorant as she was of *some* of my opinions, of my sensations (for *unlimited* confidence is requisite for the existence of mutual love)—to have some doubts, some fears? Besides, when in her natural character, her spirits are good, her conversation animated; and she was almost, in consequence, ignorant of the refinements in love which can only be attained by solitary reflection.

Forsake her! Forsake one whom I loved! Can I? Never!—But she is gone—she is lost to me for ever; for ever.

There is a mystery which I dare not to clear up; it is the only point on which I will be reserved to you. I have tried the methods you would have recommended. I followed her. I would have followed her to the end of the earth, but—— If you value the little happiness which yet remains, do not mention again to me sorrows which, if you could share in, would wound a heart which it now shall be my endeavour to heal of those pains which, through sympathy with me, it has already suffered.

I will crush Intolerance! I will, at least, attempt it. To *fail* even in so useful an attempt were glorious.

I enclose some poetry :—*

---

* The correct title of this poem, it seems, is *On an Icicle that clung to the Grass of a Grave,*—not *The Tear,* as formerly printed in editions of Shelley's

Oh! take the pure gem to where southerly
  breezes,
  Waft repose to some bosom as faithful as
    fair,
In which the warm current of love never
  freezes,
  As it rises unmingled with selfishness there,
Which, untainted by pride, unpolluted by care,
Might dissolve the dim icedrop, might bid it
  arise,
Too pure for these regions, to gleam in the
  skies.

Or where the stern warrior, his country defend-
  ing,
  Dares fearless the dark-rolling battle to
    pour,
Or o'er the fell corpse of a dread tyrant bend-
  ing,
  Where patriotism red with his guilt-reeking
    gore
Plants liberty's flag on the slave-peopled shore,
With victory's cry, with the shout of the free,
Let it fly, taintless spirit, to mingle with thee.

For I found the pure gem, when the daybeam
  returning,
  Ineffectual gleams on the snow-covered plain,

---

poems. The true title explains sufficiently the mean-
ing of the first few lines in a composition without much
value other than biographical.

L.

*When to others the wished-for arrival of morn-
ing*
  *Brings relief to long visions of soul-racking
  pain ;*
But regret is an insult—to grieve is in vain :
And why should we grieve that a spirit so fair
*Seeks Heaven to mix with its own kindred
  there ?*

*But still 'twas some spirit of kindness descend-
ing*
  To share in the load of mortality's woe,
Who over thy lowly-built sepulchre bending
  Bade sympathy's tenderest tear-drop to flow.
Not for thee, *soft compassion, celestials did
  know,*
But if angels *can weep, sure* man *may repine,*
*May weep in mute grief o'er thy low-laid
  shrine.*

And did I then say, for the altar of glory,
  *That the earliest, the loveliest of flowers I'd
  entwine,*
*Tho' with millions of blood-reeking victims
  'twas gory,*
  *Tho' the tears of the widow polluted its
  shrine,*
*Tho' around it the orphans, the fatherless
  pine ?*
Oh ! Fame, all thy glories I'd yield for a tear
To shed on the grave of a heart so sincere.

I am very cold this morning, so you must excuse bad writing, as I have been most of the night pacing a churchyard. I must now engage in scenes of strong interest.

You see the subject of the foregoing. I send it, because it may amuse you. Your letter has just arrived ; I will send W——'s * to University, when I can collect them. If it amuses you, you can answer him ; if not, I will.

I will consider your argument against the Non-existence of a Deity. Do you allow that some *supernatural* power actuates the organization of physical causes ? It is evident so far as this, that, if *power* and *wisdom* are employed in the continual arrangement of these affairs, this power, &c., is something out of the comprehension of man, as he now exists ; at least if we allow that the soul is *not* matter. Then, admitting that this actuating principle is

* See *ante*, pp. 7 and 32.

such as I have described, admitting it to be finite, there must be something beyond this, which influences *its* actions; and all this series advancing (as, if it does in one instance, it must to infinity) must at last terminate, in the existence which may be called a Deity. And, *if* this Deity thus influences the actions of the Spirits (if I may be allowed the expression) which take care of minor events (supposing your theory to be true), why is it *not* the soul of the Universe? in what is it not analogous to the soul of man? Why too is *not* gravitation the soul of a clock? I entertain no doubt of the fact, although it possesses no capabilities of variation. If the principle of life (that of reason put out of the question, as in the cases of dogs, horses, and oysters) be *soul*, then gravitation is as much the soul of a clock as animation is that of an oyster. I think we may not inaptly define *Soul* as "the most supreme, superior, and distinguished abstract appendage to the nature of anything."

But I will write again : my head is rather dizzy to-day, on account of not taking rest, and a slight attack of typhus.

Adieu, I will write soon.

Your sincerest

PERCY B. SHELLEY.*

To T. J. Hogg,
University College,
Oxford.

---

* The morbid passage at the top of page 39, about pacing a churchyard all night, is interesting in so far as it may have been the recollection of that incident which furnished the poet with the germ of the fine lines in *Alastor*—

I have made my bed
In charnels and on coffins, where black death
Keeps record of the trophies won from thee,
Hoping to still these obstinate questionings
Of thee and thine, by forcing some lone ghost
Thy messenger, to render up the tale
Of what we are.

LETTER VIII.

———

FIELD PLACE,
HORSHAM, SUSSEX.
January 11th, 1811.
[*Friday.*]

MY DEAR FRIEND,

I will not now consider your little
Essay, which arrived this morning; I
wait till to-morrow. It coincides exactly with Elizabeth's sentiments on
the subject, to whom I read it. Indeed
it has convinced her; although, from
my having a great deal to do to-day, I
cannot listen to so full an exposition
of her sentiments on the subject as I
would wish to send you. I shall write
to you to-morrow on this matter; and,
if you clear up some doubts which yet

remain, dissipate some hopes relative to the perfectibility of man, generally considered as well as individually, I will willingly submit to the system,— which at present I cannot but strongly reprobate.

How can I find words to express my thanks for such generous conduct with regard to my sister?* With talents and attainments such as you possess, to promise what I ought not perhaps to have required, what nothing but a dear sister's intellectual improvement could have induced me to demand! What can I say on the subject of your letter concerning Elizabeth? is it not dictated by the most generous and disinterested of human motives? I have not shown it to her yet; I need not explain the reason. On this point you know all.

---

* The words " generous conduct " must refer to the inditing and despatching of the " Little Essay," for the clearing up of some of Elizabeth's hazy speculative ideas—and a general promise of intellectual aid to her.

There is only one affair * of which I
will make the least cloud of mystery;
it is the only point on which I will be a
solitary being.   To be solitary, to be
reserved, in communicating pain, surely
cannot be criminal; it cannot be contrary to the strictest duties of friendship.

She is gone !   She is lost to me for
ever !   She is married ! †   Married to
a clod of earth !   She will become as
insensible herself; all those fine capabilities will moulder !

Let us speak no more on the subject.   Do not deprive me of the little
remains of peace which yet linger, that

* No doubt the *affaire de cœur* with Miss Harriet
Grove.

† This letter announces that Harriet Grove "is
married.". But it appears that in fact she did not
marry until about August of the same year [see
Rossetti's *Memoir of Shelley*, p. 26]. The letter seems
to be correctly dated in January, and the discrepancy
is a startling one.   Perhaps the likeliest way of account-
ing for it is to suppose that Shelley, in saying that
Harriet Grove was married, really meant that she had
definitely engaged herself to marry, and was therefore
virtually married.   Or perhaps the words *to be* have
been accidentally omitted in transcription.

which arises from endeavours to make others happy.

The Poetry which I sent you alluded not to the subject of my nonsensical ravings. I hope that you are now publishing one of your tales. L. * would do it, as well as any one; if you do not choose to *publish* a book at Oxford, you can *print* it there, and I will *engage* to dispose of five hundred copies. S—— professes to be acquainted with your family; *hinc illæ lacrymæ !*

I attempted to enlighten my father. *Mirabile dictu*, he for a moment listened to my arguments. He allowed the impossibility (considered abstractedly) of any preternatural interferences by Providence : he allowed the utter incredibility of witches, ghosts, legendary miracles. But, when I came to *apply* the truths on which we had agreed so harmoniously, he started at the bare

* See p. 5.

N

idea of some facts, generally believed, never having existed, and silenced me with an equine argument ; in effect with these words—" I believe, because I do not believe."

My mother imagines me to be on the high road to Pandemonium ; she fancies I want to make a deistical côterie of all my little sisters : how laughable !

You must be very solitary at Oxford. I wish I could come there now ; but, for reasons which I will tell you at meeting, it is delayed for a fortnight. I have a Poem * with Mr. L——, which I shall certainly publish ; there is some of Elizabeth's in it. I will write to-morrow. I have something to add to it ; and, if L—— has any idea, when he speaks to you, of publishing it with my name, will you tell him to leave it alone till I come.

---

* This "Poem" may very probably have been the introuvable *Poetical Essay on the Existing State of Things.*

Yes! the arms of Britannia victorious are
  bearing
    Fame, triumph, and glory, wherever they
    speed,
Her Lion his crest o'er the nations is rearing.
    Ruin follows, it tramples the dying and
    dead,
Thy countrymen fall, the blood-reeking bed
    Of the battle-slain sends a complaint-breath-
    ing sigh,
    It is mixed with the shoutings of Victory.

Old Ocean to shrieks of despair is resounding,
    It washes the terror-struck nations with
    gore,
Wild Horror the fear-palsied earth is astound-
    ing,
    And murmurs of fate fright the dread con-
    vulsed shore.
The Andes in sympathy start at the roar,
    Vast Ætna, alarmed, leans his flame-glow-
    ing brow,
    And huge Teneriffe stoops with his pinnacled
    snow.

The ice mountains echo, the Baltic, the Ocean,
    Where Cold sits enthroned on his column of
    snows,
Even Spitzbergen perceives the terrific commo-
    tion,

*The roar floats on the whirlwind of sleet, as
this blows
Blood tinges the streams as half-frozen they
flow,
The meteors of war lurid flame thro' the
air,
They mix their bright gleam with the red
polar star.*

*   *   *   *

*All are brethren, and even the African bending
To the stroke of the hard-hearted English-
man's rod,
The courtier at Luxury's palace attending,
The senator trembling at Tyranny's nod,
Each nation which kneels at the footstool of
God,
All are brethren—then banish distinction
afar,
Let Concord and Love heal the miseries of
War!*

These are Elizabeth's. She has
written many more, and I will show
you at some future time the whole of
the composition. I like it very much,

if a brother may be allowed to praise a sister. I will write to-morrow.

Yours with affection,

P. B. S.

Can you read this?

To T. J. Hogg,
University College,
Oxford.

/

O

LETTER IX.

FIELD PLACE,
HORSHAM, SUSSEX.
January 12*th*, 1811.
[*Saturday.*]

MY DEAR FRIEND,

Your letter, with the extremely beautiful enclosed poetry, came this morning. It is really admirable; it touches the heart : but I must be allowed to offer *one* critique upon it. You will be surprised to hear that I think it unfinished. You have not said that the ivy, after it had destroyed the oak, as if to mock the miseries which it caused, twined around a pine which stood near.* It is true, therefore, but does not comprehend the whole truth. As to the stuff which I sent you, I write all my poetry of that kind from the feelings of the moment ; if therefore it neither has allusion to the sentiments which rationally might be supposed to possess me, or to those which my situation might awaken, it is another proof of that egotizing variability, which I shudder to reflect how much I am in its power.

To *you* I dare represent myself as I am : wretched to the last degree. Sometimes one gleam of hope, one faint solitary gleam, seems to illumine the darkened prospect before me—but it has vanished. I fear it will never return. My sister will, I fear, never return the attachment which would once again bid me be calm. Yes ! In this alone

---

* This may possibly imply an embittered reference to the affair of Miss Grove : she being shadowed forth in the ivy, Shelley in the oak, and her husband in the pine.

is my feeble anticipation of peace placed! But what am I? Am I not the most degraded of deceived enthusiasts? Do I not deceive myself? I never, never can feel peace again!

What necessity is there for continuing in existence? " But Heaven! Eternity! Love!" My dear friend, I am yet a sceptic on these subjects: would that I could believe them to be as they are represented; would that I could totally disbelieve them!—But no! That would be selfish. I still have firmness enough to resist this last, this most horrible of errors. Is my despair the result of the hot sickly love which inflames the admirers of Sterne or Moore?* It is the conviction of unmerited unkindness; the conviction that, should a future world exist, the object of my attachment would be as miserable as myself, is the cause of it.

* *Not* Thomas Moore, but Dr. John Moore, author of *Zeluco* and *Mordaunt*.

I here take God (and a God exists) to witness, that I wish torments which beggar the futile description of a fancied hell would fall upon me, provided I could obtain thereby that happiness for what I love which, I fear, can never be ! The question is, What do I love ? It is almost unnecessary to answer. Do I love the person, the embodied identity, if I may be allowed the expression ? No ! I love what is superior, what is excellent, or what I conceive to be so ; and I wish, ardently wish, to be profoundly convinced of the existence of the Deity, that so superior a spirit might derive some degree of happiness from my feeble exertions : for love is heaven, and heaven is love. You think so too, and you disbelieve not the existence of an eternal, omnipresent Spirit.

Am I not mad ? Alas ! I am ; but I pour out my ravings into the ear of a friend who will pardon them.

P

Stay! I have an idea. I think I can prove the existence of a Deity—a First Cause. I will ask a materialist, How came this universe at first? He will answer, "By chance." What chance? I will answer in the words of Spinoza: "An infinite number of atoms had been floating from all eternity in space, till at last one of them fortuitously diverged from its track, which, dragging with it another, formed the principle of gravitation, and in consequence the universe." What cause produced this change, this chance? For where do we know that causes arise without their correspondent effects? At least we must here, on so abstract a subject, reason analogically. Was not this then a *cause*, was it not a *first* cause? Was not this first cause a Deity? Now nothing remains but to prove that this Deity has a care; or rather that its only employment consists in regulating the present and future

happiness of its creation. Our ideas
of infinite space, &c. are scarcely to be
called ideas, for we cannot either comprehend or explain them ; therefore the
Deity must be judged by us from attri-
butes analogical to our situation. Oh
that this Deity were the soul of the
universe, the spirit of universal, im-
perishable love ! Indeed I believe
it is.

But now to your argument of the
necessity of Christianity. I am not
sure that your argument does not tend
to prove its unreality. If it does not,
—you allow, you say, that love is the
only true source of rational happiness.
One man is capable of it ; why not all ?

The cullibility of man preterite I
allow ; but because men are and have
been cullible, I see no reason why they
should always continue so. Have there
not been fluctuations in the opinions
of mankind ? and, as the *stuff* which
soul is made of must be in every one

the same, would not an extended system of rational and moral unprejudiced
education render each individual capable of experiencing that degree of
happiness to which each ought to
aspire, more for others than self?

Hideous, hated traits of Superstition!
Oh Bigots! how I abhor your influence!
They are all bad enough.   But do we
not see Fanaticism decaying?   Is not
its influence weakened, except where
Faber, Rowland Hill, and several
others of the Armageddon heroes,
maintain their posts with all the
obstinacy of long-established dogma-
tism?   How I pity them! how I
despise, hate them !

Stockdale knows Mr. D. would
publish your tale.   I am beyond mea-
sure anxious for its appearance.

Adieu. Excuse my mad arguments ;
they are none at all, for I am rather
confused,—and fear, in consequence
of a fever, they will not allow me

to come * on the 26th; but I *will*. Adieu.

Your affectionate friend,

P. B. S.

You can enclose to Timothy Shelley, Esq., M.P.

To T. J. Hogg,
  University College,
    Oxford.

* To Oxford, no doubt, *via* London.

Q

LETTER X.

FIELD PLACE,
HORSHAM, SUSSEX.
January 14th, 1811.
[*Monday.*]

MY DEAR FRIEND,

Your letter and that of W——* came to-day ; yours is excellent, and, I think, will fully (in his own mind) convince Mr. W——. I enclosed five sheets of paper full this morning, and sent them to the coach with yours. I sat up all night to finish them. They attack his hypothesis in its very basis, which, at some future time, I will explain to you ; and I have attempted to prove, from the *existence* of a Deity and of Revelation, the futility of the supersti-

* See pp. 7, 32, and 39.

tion upon which he founds his whole scheme.

I was sorry to see that you even remotely suspected me of being offended with you. How I wish that I could persuade you that it is impossible !

I am really sleepy. Could you suppose that I should be so apathetic as *ever* to sleep again till my last slumber ? But be it so, and I shall take a walk in St. Leonard's Forest to dissipate it.

Adieu. You shall hear from me to-morrow.

Your sincere friend,

P. B. S.

Stockdale has behaved infamously to me : he has abused the confidence I reposed in him in sending him my work ; and he has made very free with your character, of which he knows nothing, with my father. I shall call on Stockdale on my way, that he may explain.   May I expect to see your Tale printed ?

To T. J. Hogg,
   University College,
      Oxford.

LETTER XI.

FIELD PLACE,
HORSHAM, SUSSEX.
January 16*th*, 1811.
[*Wednesday.*]

MY DEAR FRIEND,

You will hear from me to-morrow. I have to-day scarcely time but to tell you that I do not forget you. You tell me that it will show greatness of soul to rise after such a fall as mine. Ah, what pain must I feel when I contradict the flattering view which you have taken of my character! Do I not know myself? Do I not feel the acutest poignancy of mortification, amounting to actual misery? Alas, I must, with Godwin, say that in man,

R

imperfect as he now exists, there is never a motive for action unmixed; that the best has its alloy, the worst is commingled with virtue.

What does my mortification arise from? Surely not wholly for myself, nor wholly for the happiness of the being whom I have lost. Did I know, were I convinced, that I felt for nothing but Her, no self-reproach would tell me that my pangs were disgraceful. But now, when I fear, when I feel, that, in spite of myself, regret for the high happiness I have lost is mingled with the other consideration, do I feel too that it is disgraceful, degrading!

Adieu. I will write to-morrow,

P. B. SHELLEY.

To T. J. Hogg,
University College,
Oxford.

LETTER XII.

FIELD PLACE,
HORSHAM, SUSSEX.
January 17*th*, 1811.
[*Thursday.*]

MY DEAR FRIEND,

I shall be with you as soon as possible next week. You really were at Hungerford, whether you knew it or not. You tell me nothing about the tale which you promised me. I hope it gets on in the press. I am anxious for its appearance.

Stockdale certainly behaved in a vile manner to me; no other bookseller would have violated the confidence reposed in him. I will talk to him in London, where I shall be on Tuesday. Can I do anything for you there ?

You notice the peculiarity of the expression " My Sister " in my letters.* It certainly arose independent of consideration, and I am happy to hear that it is so.

Your systematic cudgel for blockheads is excellent. I tried it on with my father, who told me that thirty years ago he had read Locke, but this made no impression. The "*equus et res*" are all that I can boast of; the "*pater*" is swallowed up in the first article of the catalogue.

You tell me nothing of the tale ; I am all anxiety about it. I am forced hastily to bid you adieu.

P. B. SHELLEY.

To T. J. Hogg,
 University College,
  Oxford.

---

* The " peculiarity " was, presumably, that Shelley who had four sisters, spoke of " my sister "—Elizabeth —as if he had only one. See note at p. 14.

LETTER XIII.

FIELD PLACE,
HORSHAM, SUSSEX.
[*January 23rd*, 1811.
Wednesday.]

MY DEAR FRIEND,

You are all over the country. I shall be at Oxford on Friday or Saturday evening. I will write to you from London.

My father's prophetic prepossession in your favour is become as high as before it was to your prejudice. Whence it arises, or from what cause, I am inadequate to say; I can merely state the fact. He came from London full of your praises; your family, that of Mr. Hogg, of Norton House, near

s

Stockton-upon-Tees. Your principles
are *now* as divine as before they were
diabolical. I tell you this with extreme
satisfaction, and, to sum up the whole,
he has desired me to make his compli-
ments to you, and to invite you to
make Field Place your head-quarters
for the Easter vacation. I hope you
will accept of it. I fancy he has been
talking in town to some of the northern
Members of Parliament who are acquainted with your family. However
that may be, I hope you have no other
arrangement for Easter which can in-
terfere with granting me the pleasure of
introducing you personally here.

You have very well drawn your line
of distinction between instinctive and
rational motives of action. The *former*
are not in our own power. Yet we
may doubt if even these are *purely*
selfish,—as congeniality, sympathy, un-
accountable attractions of intellect,
which arise independent frequently of

any considerations of your own interest, operating violently in contradiction
to it, and bringing on wretchedness,
which your reason plainly foresees,—
which yet, although your judgment dis-
[ap]proves of, you take no pains to ob-
viate. All this is not selfish. And surely
the operations of reason, of judgment,
in a man whose judgment is fully convinced of the baseness of any motive,
can never be consonant with it.

Adieu. Your affectionate,

P. B. SHELLEY.

To T. J. Hogg,
University College,
Oxford.

LETTER XIV.

To JOHN HOGG, ESQ.*

———

15, POLAND STREET,
LONDON.

[*April*, 1811.]

SIR,

I accompanied (at his desire) Mr.
Jefferson Hogg to Mr. C., who was
entrusted with certain propositions to
be offered to my friend. I was there
extremely surprised—no less hurt than
surprised—to find my father, in his
interview with Mr. C., had, either un-
advisedly or intentionally, let fall ex-

* Father of T. Jefferson Hogg.

pressions which conveyed an idea
that Mr. Jefferson Hogg was the
"original corruptor" of my principles.
That on this subject (notwithstanding
his long experience) Mr. T. Shelley
must know less than his son, will be
conceded; and I feel it but justice
(in consequence of your feelings, so
natural after what Mr. C. communi-
cated) positively to deny the assertion.
I feel this tribute, which I have paid
to the just sense of horror you entertain, to be due to you as a gentleman.
I hope my motives stand excused to
your candour.

Myself and my friend have offered
concessions *; painful, indeed, they are
to myself, but such as on mature consideration we find due to our high
sense of filial duty.

Permit me to request your indul-

---

* Concessions relating (at all events in part) to the
conditions under which the intimacy between Hogg
and Shelley was to be continued henceforward.

T

gence for the liberty I have taken in thus addressing you.

I remain your obedient humble servant,

P. B. SHELLEY.*

To John Hogg, Esq.,
    Norton,
        Stockton-on-Tees.

---

* In the interval between the despatch of letter No. XIII. and letter No. XV. much had happened. Shelley had at length rejoined Hogg at College; and the tendency of the two youthful minds towards audacity of enquiry, so evident in this correspondence, had blossomed out into that portentous tract *The Necessity of Atheism.* This, though issued anonymously, was known to be by Shelley, who indeed distributed copies ostentatiously. Questioned by the Master of University College as to the authorship, he declined to answer. Hogg was questioned in like manner, and in like manner refused information. On the 25th of March, 1811, both youths were summarily expelled, not, ostensibly, for the publication of the tract, but for contumaciously refusing to answer questions. They went together to London and lodged together; but before the next letter was written, not only had Hogg left London, but Shelley had become acquainted with Harriet Westbrook, her sister Eliza, and her father, a retired coffee-house keeper,—Harriet being then sixteen years old, and at the Clapham school where the Misses Shelley were resident.

LETTER XV.

—————

15, POLAND STREET,
LONDON.
April 18*th*, 1811.
[*Thursday.*]

MY DEAR FRIEND,

Certainly this place is a little solitary; but, as a person cannot be quite alone when he has even got himself with him, I get on pretty well. I have employed myself in writing poetry; and, as I go to bed at eight o'clock, time passes quicker than it otherwise might.

Yesterday I had a letter from Whitton * to invite me to his house; of course, the answer was negative. I

* Whitton was the legal adviser of Mr. Timothy Shelley.

wrote to say that I would resign all claim to the entail, if he * would allow me two hundred pounds a-year, and divide the rest among my sisters. Of course he will not refuse the offer.

You remark that, in Lord Mount Edgecumbe's hermitage, I should have nothing to talk of but myself; nor have I anything here, except I should transcribe the *jeux-d'esprit* of the maid.

Mr. Pilfold has written a very civil letter; my mother intercepted that† sent to my father, and wrote to me to come, enclosing the money. I, of course, returned it.

Miss Westbrook has this moment called on me, with her sister. It certainly was very kind of her.

Adieu. The post goes.

Yours,

P. B. S.

To T. J. Hogg,
　　Ellesmere.

---

* The reference here is, of course, to Shelley's father.
† Probably a letter by Shelley repeating his offer re £200.

LETTER XVI.

———

LONDON.
April 24th, 1811.
[*Wednesday.*]

MY DEAR FRIEND,

You have (with wonderful sagacity, no doubt) refuted an argument of mine, the very existence of which I had forgotten. Something singularly conceited, no doubt, by the remarks you make on it. "Fine flowery language," you say. Well, I cannot help it: you see me in my weakest moments. All I can tell you of it is that I certainly was not "laughing," as you conjecture. This circumstance may go *against* me. I do not know that it will, however, as I have by no

U

means a *precise* idea of what the subject of this composition was.

"The Galilean is not a favourite of mine," a French author writes. (The French write audaciously — rashly.) "So far from owing him any thanks for his favours, I cannot avoid confessing that I owe a secret grudge to his carpentership (*charpenterie*). The reflecting part of the community—that part in whose happiness we philosophers have so strong an interest—certainly do not require his morality, which, where there is no *vice*, fetters *virtue*. Here we all agree. Let this horrid Galilean rule the *Canaille* then ! I give them up." And *I* give them up. I will no more mix politics and virtue, they are incompatible.*

* I think this remark must arise out of some considerations set forth in Godwin's *Political Justice*, to the effect that virtue can be promoted by political institution. Shelley, it is evident, had heretofore rallied to that opinion ; but he now, after discussion with Hogg, relinquishes it. Who was this "French author"?—Voltaire, or one of that connection?

My little friend Harriet Westbrook is gone to her prison-house.* She is quite well in health; at least so she says, though she looks very much otherwise. I saw her yesterday. I went with her and her sister to Miss H.'s,† and walked about Clapham Common with them for two hours. The youngest is a most amiable girl; ·the eldest, is really conceited, but very condescending. I took the sacrament with her on Sunday. ‡

You say I talk philosophically of her "kindness" in calling on me. She is very charitable and good. § I shall always think of it with gratitude, because I certainly did not deserve it, and she exposed herself to much possible odium. It is scarcely doing her a kindness—it is perhaps inducing

* Mrs. Fenning's school at Clapham.
† Apparently some friend of the Westbrook's, residing near Harriet's schoolhouse.
‡ *April* 21*st,* 1811.
§ "She" must, to judge from the general context, mean *Harriet*: though it seems at first sight rather to mean her sister *Eliza,* the *elder* Miss Westbrook.

positive unhappiness—to point out to
her a road which leads to perfection,
the attainment of which, perhaps, does
not repay the difficulties of the pro-
gress. What do you think of this?
If trains of thought, development of
mental energies, influence in any
degree a future state; if this is *even*
possible—if it stands on *at all* securer
ground than mere hypothesis; then is
it not a service?—Where am I gotten?
Perhaps into another ridiculous argument. I will not proceed; for I shall
forget all I have said, and cannot, in
justice, animadvert upon any of your
critiques.

I called on John Grove * this morning. I met my father in the passage,
and politely enquired after his health.
He looked as black as a thunder-cloud,
and said " Your most humble servant! "
I made him a low bow, and, wishing

* A cousin of Shelley's, and brother of Harriet
Grove, living in Lincoln's Inn.

him a very good morning, passed on.
He is very irate about my proposals.*
I cannot resign anything till I am
twenty-one. I cannot do anything;
therefore I have three more years
to consider of the matter you mentioned.

I shall go down to Field Place soon.
I wait for Mr. Pilfold's arrival, with
whom I shall depart. He is resolved
(the old fellow) that I shall not stay at
Field Place. If I please—as I shall
do for some time—I *will.* This reso-
lution of mine was hinted to him :
"Oh, then I shall take his sister away
before he comes." But I shall follow
her, as her retirement cannot be a
secret. This will probably lead me
to wander about for some time. You
will hear from me, however, wherever
I am.

If all these things are useless, you

---

* The " proposals " as to money-matters—mentioned
in the preceding letter.

will see me at York, or at Ellesmere if you still remain there. "The scenery excites mournful ideas." I am sorry to hear it ; I hoped that it would have had a contrary effect. May I indulge the idea that York is as stupid as Oxford? And yet you did not wander *alone* amid the mountains. I think I shall live at the foot of Snowdon. Suppose we both go there directly. Do not be surprised if you see me at Ellesmere. Yes, you would, for it would be a strange thing. I am now nearly recovered.*

Strange that Florian could not see the conclusions from his own reasoning! How can the hope of a higher reward, stimulating the action, make it virtuous, if the essence of virtue is disinterested ? as all, who know anything of virtue, must allow, as *he* does allow. How inconsistent is this religion ! How

---

* "Recovered," it would seem, from a college strain. See letter dated *April 29th*, 1811.

apt to pervert the judgment, and finally
the heart, of the most amiably-inten-
tioned who confide in it !

I wish I was with you in the mountains ; could not we live there ?

Direct to 15 Poland Street.   I write
to-morrow to York.   :

Your affectionate friend,

P. B. S.

Your B——* is worse than stupid ;
he is provoking.   Have you really
no one to associate with—not even a
peasant, a child of nature, a spider ?
" And this from the hermit, the philosopher ! "   Oh, you are right to laugh
at me !

I finished the little poem, one stanza
of which you said was pretty ; it is, on
the whole, a most stupid thing, as you
will confess when I some day inflict a

---

* Apparently the college friend with whom Hogg had
left London, and gone to Ellesmere.   Was he the
Burdon mentioned elsewhere in Shelley's correspondence ?

perusal of it on your innocent ears. Yet I have nothing to amuse myself with ; and, if it does not injure others, and you cannot avoid it, I do not see much harm in being mad. You even vindicate it in some almost inspired stanzas, which I found among my transcriptions to-day.

Adieu, I am going to Miss West-brook's to dinner. Her father is out. I will write to-morrow.*.

> *To T. J. Hogg,*
>   *Ellesmere.*

---

* No letter written upon the following day, *April 25th,* 1811, is at present forthcoming. It is evident from the last paragraph of the foregoing that Eliza, aged 30 or so, and Harriet, aged 16, were at least not averse to a little defiance of Mrs. Grundy. Hence, still smarting from the loss of Harriet Grove and breathing out threatenings and slaughter against Intolerance, Shelley gladly seized a chance of obtaining, as he thought, colleagues in his warfare. See especially p. 90.

·LETTER XVII.

15, Poland Street,
London.
April 26th, 1811.
[*Friday.*]

My dear Friend,

I indulge despair. *Why* do I so? I will not philosophize. It is perhaps a poor way of administering comfort to myself to say that I *ought* not to be in need of it. I fear the despair which springs from disappointed love is a passion,—a passion, too, which is least of all reducible to reason. But it is a passion, it is independent of volition; it is the necessary effect of a cause, which *must*, I feel, continue to operate. Wherefore, then, do you ask *Why* I

Y

indulge despair? And what shall I tell you which can make you happier, which can alleviate even solitude and regret? Shall I tell you the truth? Oh you are too well aware of that, or you would not talk of despair! Shall I say that the time may come when happiness shall dawn upon a night of wretched-ness? Why should I be a false prophet if I said this? I do not know, except on the general principle that the evils in this world powerfully overbalance its pleasures; how, then, could I be justi-fied in saying this? You will tell me to cease to think, to cease to feel; you will tell me to be anything but what I am; and I feel I must obey the com-mand before I can talk of hope.

I find there can be bigots in philo-sophy as well as in religion; I, per-haps, may be classed with the former. I *have* read your letter attentively. Yet *all* religionists *do* judge of philosophers in the way which you reprehend. *Faith*

is one of the highest moral virtues,—
the foundation, indeed, upon which all
others must rest ; and religionists think
that he who has neglected to *cultivate*
this has not performed *one third* of the
moral duties, as Bishop Warburton dog-
matically asserts. The religionists, then,
by this very *Faith*, without which they
could not be religionists, think the most
virtuous philosopher must have neglected one third of the moral duties !

If, then, a religionist, the *most* amiable of them, regards the best philosopher as *far* from being virtuous, has
not a philosopher reason to suspect the
amiability of a system which inculcates
so glaringly uncharitable opinions ?
Can a being amiable to a high degree
—possessed, of course, of judgment,
without which amiability would be in
a poor way—hold such opinions as
these ? Supposing even they were sup-
ported by reason, they ought to be
suspected as leading to a conclusion

ad absurdum; since, however, they combine irrationality and absurdity with effects on the mind most opposite to retiring amiability, are they not to be *more* than suspected? Take any system of religion, lop off all the disgusting excrescences, or rather adjuncts; retain virtuous precepts; qualify selfish dogmas (I would even allow as much irrationality as amiability could swallow, but uncombined with immorality and self-conceitedness); do all this, and *I* will say, It is a system which *can* do no harm, and, indeed, is highly requisite for the vulgar. But perhaps it is best for the latter that *they* should have it as their fathers gave it them; that the amiable, the enquiring should reject it altogether.

Yet I will allow that it *may* be consistent with amiability, when amiability does not know the deformity of the wretched errors, and that they *really* are as we behold them. I cannot judge of a system by the flowers which are scattered here and there; you omit the mention of the *weeds*, which grow so high that few botanists can see the flowers; and those who *do* gather the latter are frequently, I fear, tainted with the pestilential vapour of the former.

The argument of *supremacy* is really amiable, without that, I should give up the remotest *possibility* of success. Yet that applies but to the existence of a *Creator*, that is inconsequential: the enquirer here, the amiable enquirer, does not pause at the world, lest *she* should be left supreme; she advances *one* step higher,—not being aware, or not caring to be aware, of the infinity of the staircase which she ascends.*
This is *irrational*, but it is not unamiable,—it does not involve the hateful consequences of selfishness, self-con-

* To see exactly what Shelley meant by these somewhat nebulous phrases, we sadly need Hogg's letter.

ceitedness, and the subserviency of faith to the volition of the believer, which are necessary to the existence of " a spurious system of theology."

A *religionist*, I will allow, may be more amiable than a philosopher, although in one instance reason is allowed to sleep, that amiability may watch. Yet, my dear friend, this is not Intolerance ; nor can that odious system stand excused on this ground, as its very principle revolts against the dear modesty which suggests a dereliction of reason in the other instance. I again assert—nor perhaps are you prepared to deny, much as your amiable motion might prompt you to wish it— that religion is too often the child of cold prejudice and selfish fear. Love of a Deity, of Allah, Bramah (it is all the same), certainly springs from the latter motive ; is this *love ?* You know too well it is not. Here I appeal to your own heart, your own feelings. At

that tribunal I feel that I am secure.
I once could almost *tolerate* intolerance,—it then merely injured me.
Once it merely deprived *me* of all
that I cared for, touching myself, on
earth ; but now it has done more, and
I cannot forgive.

Eloisa said ; "I have hated myself,
that I might love thee, Abelard."
When I hear a religionist prepared
to say so, as her sincere sentiments,
I then will allow that in a *few* in-
stances the virtue of religion is separ-
able from the vice.

" She is *not* lost for ever "! How I
hope that may be true ! But I fear
I can never ascertain, I can never
influence an amelioration, as she does
not any longer permit a " *philosopher* "
to correspond with her. She talks of
duty to her *Father*. And this is your
amiable religion !

You will excuse my raving, my dear
friend : you will not be severe upon my

hatred of a cause which can produce such an effect as this.

You talk of the dead : " Do we not exist after the tomb ? "—It is a natural question, my friend, when there is nothing in life : yet it is one on which you have never told me any *solid* grounds for your opinions.

You shall hear from me again soon. I send some verses. I heard from F. yesterday. All that he said was : " My letters are arrived.—G. S. F."

My dear friend,
Your affectionate,
P. B. SHELLEY.

LETTER XVIII.

LINCOLN'S INN FIELDS,
LONDON.
April, 28*th*, 1811.
[*Sunday.*]

MY DEAR FRIEND,

I am now at Grove's. I don't know where I am, where I will be. Future, present, past, is all a mist : it seems as if I had begun existence anew, under auspices so unfavourable. Yet no ! That is stupid.

My poor little friend * has been ill : her sister sent for me the other night. I found her on a couch, pale. Her father is civil to me, very strangely : the sister is too civil by half. She

* Harriet Westbrook.

A A

began talking about *l'Amour*. I philo-
sophized : and the youngest said she
had such a headache that she could
not bear conversation   Her sister then
went away, and I stayed till half-past
twelve. Her father had a large party
below, he invited me : I refused.

Yes! The fiend, the wretch, shall
fall!* Harriet will do for one of
the crushers, and the eldest (Emily), †
with some taming, will do, too. They
are both very clever, and the youngest
(my friend) is amiable. Yesterday she
was better. To-day her father compelled her to go to Clapham, whither I
have conducted her ; and I am now returned.

Why is it that, the moment we two
are separated, I can scarcely set bounds
to my hatred of intolerance? Is it feeling? is it passion ? I would willingly

---

* " The fiend, the wretch " = Intolerance.
† " Emily " can only have been Eliza. Possibly
the elder Miss Westbrook may have borne *both* names,
though the latter is the only one that has been recorded.

persuade myself that it is neither ; willingly would I persuade myself that all
that is amiable, all that is good, falls by
its prevalence, and that *I* ought un-
ceasingly to attempt its destruction.
Yet you say that millions of bad are
necessary for the existence of a few
pre-eminent in excellence.   Is not this
a despotism of virtue, which is inconsistent with its nature ?   Is it not the
Asiatic tyrant who renders his territory
wretched to fill his seraglio? the shark
who must glut his maw with millions of
fish in order that he may exist ?   I
have often said that I doubted your
divinities ; and, if this inference follows
the established hypothesis of their
existence, I do not merely doubt, but
hope that my doubts are founded on
truth.

I think, then, that the *term* " superior "* is bad, as it involves this horrible

* Hogg would seem to have been writing of men as
" superior " to women.

consequence. Let the word "perfect,"
then, be offered as a substitute ; to
which each who aspires may indulge
a hope of arriving ; or rather every one
(speaking of *men*) may hope to contribute to woman's arrival, which, in fact,
is themselves advancing ; although, like
the shadow preceding the figure, or the
spiral, it always may advance, and never
touch.

My sister does not come to town,
nor will she ever, at least I can see no
chance of it. I will not deceive myself ; she is lost, lost to everything ;
Intolerance has tainted her,—she talks
cant and twaddle. I would not venture
thus to prophesy without being most
perfectly convinced in my own mind of
the truth of what I say. It *may* not be
irretrievable ; but yes, it is ! A young
female who only once, only for a short
time, asserted her claim to an unfettered
use of reason, bred up with bigots, having before her eyes examples of the

consequences of scepticism,—or even of philosophy, which she must now see to lead directly to the former. A mother who is mild and tolerant, yet narrow-minded. How, I ask, is *she* to be rescued from its influence?

I tell you, my dear friend, openly the feelings of my mind, the state of its convictions on every subject ; this, then, is one, and I do not expect that you will say, " It must be so painful to your feelings that I hope you will never again mention it." I do not expect you to say : " I had rather you were under a pleasing error ; it is not a friendly act to dissipate the mists which hide a frightful prospect."

On other subjects you have soared above prejudices; you have investigated them, terrible as they may have appeared, and resolved to abide by the result of that investigation. And you *have* abided by it. Why then should there yet remain a subject on which

you profess yourself fearful to enquire?
I will not allow you to say "incom-
petent." Error cannot in any of its
shapes be good ; I cannot conceive the
possibility.

You talk of the credulity of mankind, its proneness to superstition, that
it ever has been a slave to the vilest of
errors. Is your inference necessary, or
direct, that it ever will continue so?
You say that "I have no idea how
society could be freed from false
notions on almost every subject."
No ; nor would the first man in the
world, supposing that there ever was
one, at the moment of his arriving to
his estate, have any conception how a
fertile piece of land would look without weeds. He stares at it, and thinks
it is least of all fitted for his con-
veniences ; when a stricter searching
into its nature would convince him
that it was calculated to contribute to
them, with a sufficient proportion of

labour, more than the barer land which appeared clear.

Dares the lama, most fleet of the sons of the
    wind,
  The lion to rouse from his skull-covered lair ?
When the tiger approaches, can the fast-fleet-
    ing hind
  Repose trust in his footsteps of air ?
No. Abandon'd he sinks in a trance of de-
    spair :
  The monster transfixes his prey :
  On the sand flows his life-blood away,
Whilst India's rocks to his death-yells reply,
Protracting the horrible harmony.

Yet the fowl of the desert, when danger en-
    croaches,
  Dares fearless to perish, defending her brood,
Though the fiercest of cloud-piercing tyrants
    approaches,
  Thirsting—aye thirsting—for blood,
And demands, like mankind, his brother for
    food ;—
  Yet more lenient, more gentle, than they,—
  For hunger, not glory, the prey
Must perish. Revenge does not howl o'er the
    dead,
Nor ambition with fame crown the murderer's
    head.

Though weak as the lama that bounds on the
    mountains,
And endued not with fast-fleeting footsteps of
    air,
Yet, yet will I draw from the purest of
    fountains,
    Though a fiercer than tiger is there ;
Though, more dreadful than death, it scatters
    despair,
    Though its shadow eclipses the day,
    And the darkness of deepest dismay
Spreads the influence of soul-chilling terror
    around,
And lowers on the corpses, that rot on the
    ground.

They came to the fountain to draw from its
    stream
    Waves too pure, too celestial, for mortals to
    see ;
They bathed for a while in its silvery beam,
    Then perished, and perished like me.
For in vain from the grasp of the Bigot I flee ;
    The most tenderly loved of my soul
    Are slaves to his hated control.
He pursues me, he blasts me ! 'Tis in vain
    that I fly !
What remains but to curse him,—to curse him,
    and die ?

There it is—a mad effusion of this morning !

I had resolved not to mortgage,* before you left London ; I told you that I should divide it with my sisters, and leave everything else to fate.

Your affectionate friend,

P. B. S.

* *Cf.* p. 72.

CONTENTS.

CONTENTS.

VOL. I.

———

VOL. I.   *b*

LETTERS

FROM

PERCY BYSSHE SHELLEY

TO

THOMAS JEFFERSON HOGG.

WITH NOTES BY W. M. ROSSETTI AND
H. BUXTON FORMAN.

VOLUME I.

\

London : Privately Printed.
1897.

Percy B. Shelley, William M. Rossetti, Thomas J. Wise, Henry M. Stephens, Harry B. Forman

Letters from Percy Bysshe Shelley to Thomas Jefferson Hogg
with notes by W. M. Rossetti and H. Buxton Forman

ISBN/EAN: 9783337388027

Printed in Europe, USA, Canada, Australia, Japan

Cover: Foto ©Andreas Hilbeck / pixelio.de

More available books at **www.hansebooks.com**

www.ingramcontent.com/pod-product-compliance
Lightning Source LLC
Chambersburg PA
CBHW022342020726
47500CB00004B/1238